RISE OF DRACULA

CHAPTER ONE

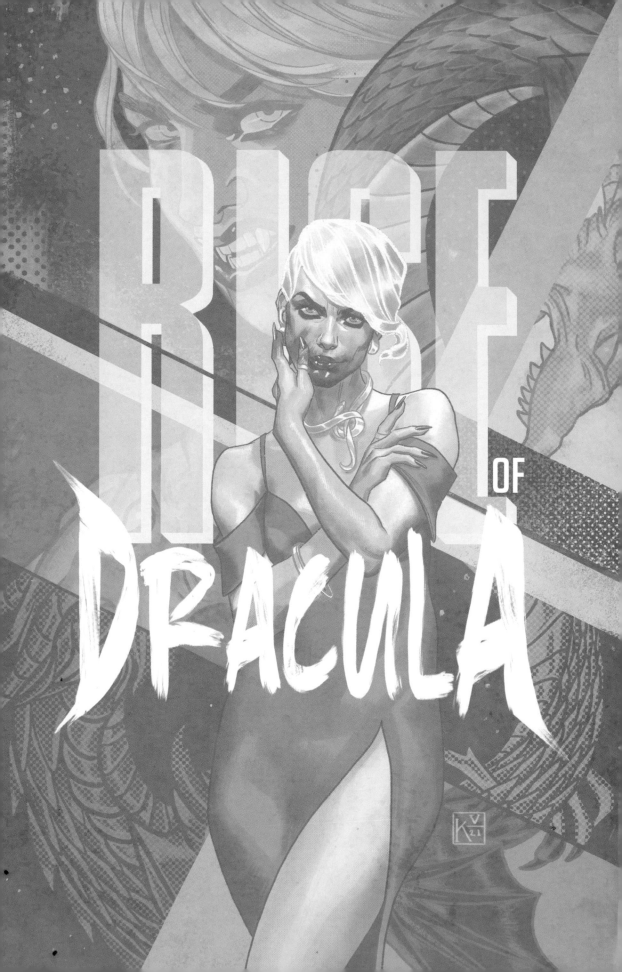

RISE OF DRACULA

INSPIRED BY
CHARACTERS CREATED
BY BRAM STOKER

**RICH
DAVIS**
WRITER/CREATOR

PU
CALZ
ART

I WARNED THEM. THEY WOULDN'T LISTEN.
THEY NEVER DO.
DA
ALEX ZIEF
COLORS
DAVE LENTZ
LETTERS/DESIGN
PAUL PITTINGER
EXECUTIVE PRODUCER
AMBER DAVIS
EDITOR

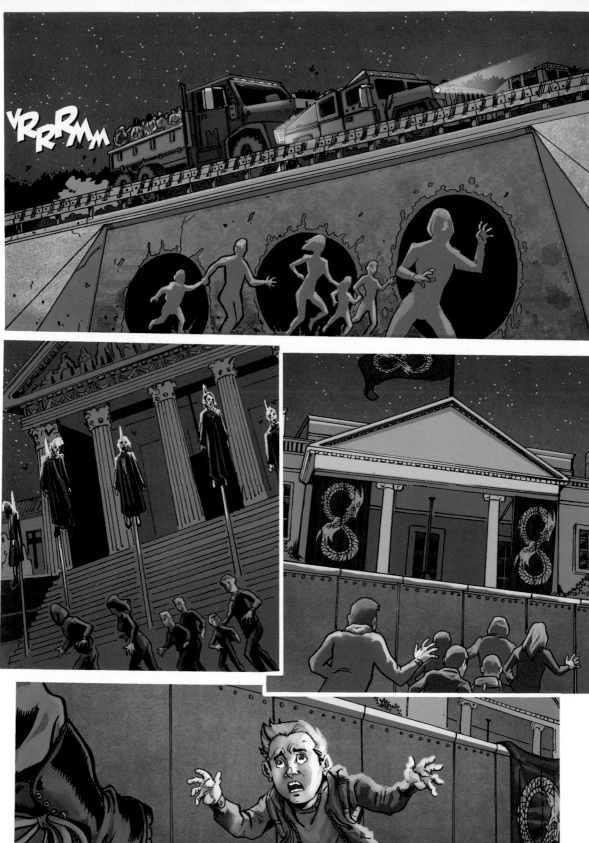

VRRRMM

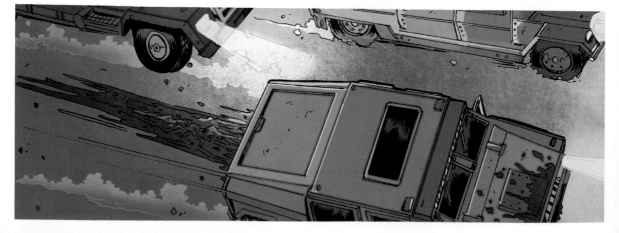

I'D LIKE TO PROVIDE A BRIEF SITUATION UPDATE BEFORE I TAKE YOUR QUESTIONS.

AS OF 0300, WE HAVE LIBERATED THE CITY OF WASHINGTON DC.

OUR PEACEKEEPERS HAVE SECURED THE PENTAGON, THE CAPITAL, THE WHITE HOUSE AND OTHER KEY OBJECTIVES.

"WE ARE NEGOTIATING A FORMAL SURRENDER WITH THE SECRETARY OF EDUCATION AS WE SPEAK.

"BEFORE SUNRISE, WE WILL HAVE RESTORED THE RULE OF LAW TO THESE UNITED STATES UNDER OUR GOVERNMENT...

"...AS SUPPORTED BY THE WILL OF THE PEOPLE.

"WHILE WE CONTINUE TO EXPERIENCE POCKETS OF MINOR RESISTANCE, WE ARE CONFIDENT THAT WE MAY NOW TURN OUR FOCUS TOWARD OUR HUMANITARIAN AGENDA."

HEY! WHAT ARE YOU--

SPLORT

EEEEW! GROSS!

GIVE 'EM HELL, BOYS!

RISE OF DRACULA

CHAPTER TWO

CARMILLA! WE HAVE A SITUATION.

SHOW ME.

TEMPLAR KNIGHTS ARE ASSAULTING A RAVE ON U-STREET.

WE HAVE URBAN ASSAULT DRONES, YES?

WE DO.

USE THEM.

WE'LL HIT OUR OWN PEOPLE.

YES, BUT WE'LL HIT THEIRS AS WELL.

WE'RE HITTING A SHIPMENT. KIDS. ON THEIR WAY TO THE FARMS.

WE'RE GETTING THEM AWAY FROM YOUR PSYCHO SISTER.

SHE'S NOT PSYCHOTIC.

SHE COMMITTED GENOCIDE.

HER METHODS SUCK...BUT SHE'S NOT WRONG.

HOW CAN YOU SAY THAT?

DO YOU HEAR SIRENS?

NO.

GUNSHOTS?

...

BREEDERS? PETS? CAN YOU HEAR YOURSELF RIGHT NOW?

HUMANS HAD TWO HUNDRED *THOUSAND* YEARS.

WHAT DID YOU DO WITH ALL THAT TIME?

YOU FOUGHT WARS. YOU *RAPED.* YOU *MURDERED.* YOU DROVE 99.9% OF EVERY *THING* THAT EVER LIVED INTO EXTINCTION.

YOU SUCKED THE PLANET DRY OF EVERY POSSIBLE RESOURCE.

YOU WERE GIVEN PARADISE AND YOU MADE IT YOUR TOILET.

I DON'T FEEL SORRY FOR YOU. WHY SHOULD I? YOU'RE A SPECIES OF PERPETUAL TODDLERS.

YOU'VE PROVEN YOU CAN'T BE LEFT ALONE.

YOU NEED CONSTANT SUPERVISION.

I'M SORRY YOU'RE HAVING TROUBLE ADJUSTING TO A NEW APEX PREDATOR, BUT YOU SHOWED US WHAT TO DO.

WE'RE JUST BETTER AT IT.

WILL YOU HELP ME?

...YES...

BLAM

BLAM

HA HA HA HA HA HA HA

I AM WAY TOO FUCKING HIGH FOR THIS!

ELLIE!

ON YOUR FEET, BITCH!

BLAM BLAM BLAM

AAAIEEEEEEEEEEE

PSST PSST

BRAKKA BRAKKA
BRAKKA
BRAKKA
BRAKKA
SPLUT
SPLUT
SPLUT

CLANG

SCHLICK

BOGGIN BAWBAG!

DRACULINA.

I NEED TO SEE MY SISTER.

I'M AFRAID THAT'S NOT POSSIBLE, DRACULINA.

WHY?

IT'S ALRIGHT, DOLORES. SEND HER IN.

OF COURSE, DRACULA.

MY APOLOGIES, DRACULINA. I WAS MISTAKEN.

THANK YOU, DOLORES.

LUCY!

SMEK

GENTLEMEN, I NEED A MOMENT WITH MY SISTER.

THIS WAY. WE'LL RECONVENE IN THE CABINET ROOM.

ONLY A MOMENT. YOU STILL HAVE THE FIVE FAMILIES AND YOUR NIGHTLY WAR BRIEFING ON THE AGENDA.

LADY RUTHVEN WANTS FIVE MINUTES BEFORE THE STATE DINNER...

THANK YOU, CARMILLA. THAT WILL BE ALL.

DRACULA.

I'M SO HAPPY YOU'RE HERE. I CAN JUST BE MINA. *FUCK* DRACULA.

I THOUGHT YOU WANTED THIS?

I DID. *I DO.* IT'S STILL A BURDEN.

EVERYONE HATES ME.

NO... MINA...

THE U.N. LABELED ME A WAR CRIMINAL. I'VE BEEN EXCOMMUNICATED, *CONDEMNED* AS TAKFIR AND THEY DECLARED CHEREM AGAINST ME.

SOMEHOW I'VE BECOME THE DEVIL AFTER I SENT THE LITERAL DEVIL *STRAIGHT TO HELL.*

WHY CAN'T THEY SEE? I'M ONLY SAVING THEM FROM THEMSELVES!

I'M SORRY.

YOU WANTED TO TALK AND HERE I AM RAMBLING ON ABOUT THINGS YOU DON'T UNDERSTAND.

BRAKKA BRAKKA BRAKKA

RRRGGHHH!

SPLUT

TSSS TSSS TSSS TSSS

WHUP WHUP WHUP

KABOW

THIS JUST IN. YOU'RE LOOKING AT A DISTURBING LIVE SHOT OF THE WAREHOUSE DISTRICT NEAR U STREET IN WASHINGTON, DC.

THE TRANSITION OF POWER IN THE UNITED STATES APPEARS LESS PEACEFUL THAN THE NEW ORDO DRACUL GOVERNMENT HAS LED US TO BELIEVE...

ARE DEMOCRATS SNEAKING NANO-SPY-BOTS INTO YOUR DRINKING WATER? FOX NEWS REPORTS. YOU DECIDE. NEXT.

WHITE HOUSE SOURCES TELL US THAT A GROUP CALLING THEMSELVES THE NEW SOLDIERS OF SOLOMON HAVE CLAIMED CREDIT FOR THIS BRUTAL ACT OF TERRORISM.

CASUALTIES ARE *WAY* BEYOND PROJECTIONS.

AND THE RUTHVEN GIRLS!?

WHAT THE *FUCK* HAPPENED ABE? WHY WERE THEY THERE?

I DON'T KNOW.

LADY RUTHVEN IS BLAMING DRACULA. IT'S ALL OVER TWITTER.

I'LL HANDLE IT.

White House

YOU'D BETTER!

WE *NEED* HER INFLUENCE. THIS ALL FALLS APART WITHOUT HER.

I AM MORE THAN AWARE.

HOW DO WE SPIN IT?

TERRORISTS. THUGS. DEVIANTS. SAME WAY WE HANDLE ANY ACTIVIST UPRISING. WE MAKE HER DAUGHTERS INTO MARTYRS.

THAT MIGHT WORK FOR BABS AND LARA. BUT...

ELLIE.

I HAVEN'T SEEN A MONSTER LIKE HER IN 400 YEARS.

SHE'S WHAT YOU'D GET IF THE JOKER AND HARLEY QUINN DID BATH SALTS AND MADE A METH ADDICTED, SCHIZOPHRENIC BABY.

THAT'S ELLIE.

THANK YOU ALL FOR COMING.

RISE OF DRACULA

CHAPTER THREE

I MAY NOT LIVE TO SEE OUR GLORY.

BUT I WILL GLADLY JOIN THE FIGHT.

AND WHEN OUR CHILDREN TELL OUR STORY--

♪THEY'LL TELL THE STORY OF TONIGHT...♪

I LOVE HAMILTON. I WISH WE COULD HAVE SEEN IT ON BROADWAY.

SOMEDAY. WHEN THIS IS ALL OVER

BORK

BORK

BORK
BORK

JESUS GODDAMN CHRIST!

BORK
BORK

HA HA HA HA HA

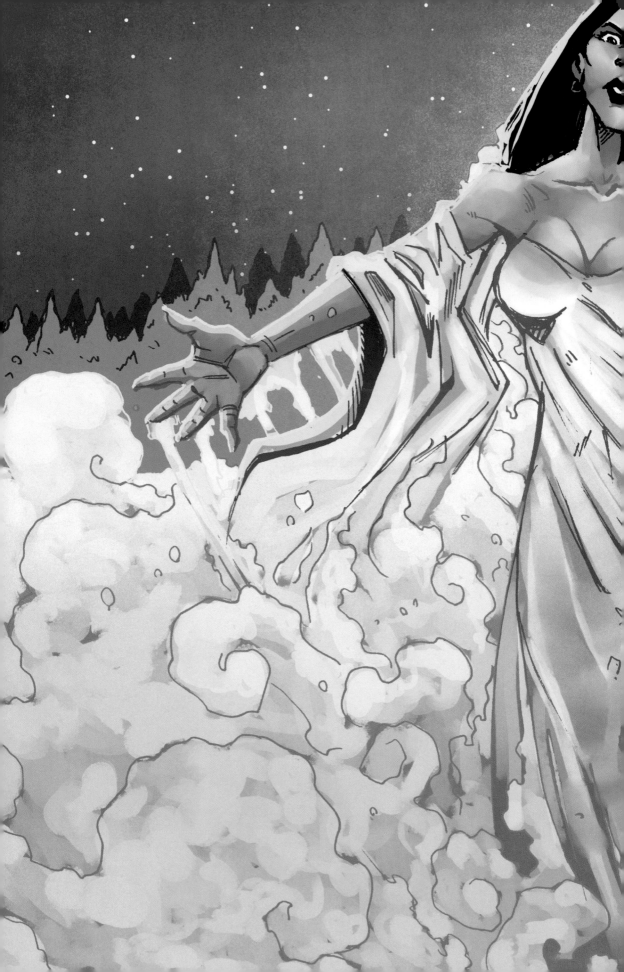

NO. NOT TONIGHT.

SHUT THE FUCK UP, SYLVIA!

SYLVIA?

PLATH? SHE STUCK HER HEAD IN AN OVEN.

YOUR HEAD'S IN A JAR.

SHE WROTE THE BELL JAR...

YOU KNOW WHAT? IF I HAVE TO EXPLAIN IT, IT'S NOT FUNNY ANYMORE.

BETTER TO RULE IN HELL THAN SERVE IN HEAVEN.

GODS-DAMNED RIGHT!

≥SIGH≤

WHAT? ARE WE SUPPOSED TO MOPE AROUND ALL SAD AND PENITENT?

FUCK THAT!

FUCK THAT!

OK, BUT SERIOUSLY, WE'VE GOTTA DO SOMETHING. WE'RE MORE THAN COMIC RELIEF... RIGHT?

LOOK AT YOU GETTING ALL EXISTENTIALLY META!

FLIP

≥SIGH≤

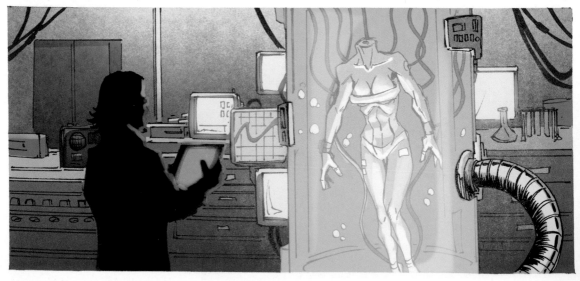

Baghras Castle, Turkey

SCREEEE

SCREEEE...

XREE

SUBJECT 01271945. ORGAN REGENERATION IS CONSISTENT WITH PREVIOUS EXPERIMENTS.

AAAIIEEE

PROGRESS, VICTOR?

MINIMAL AT BEST.

WE NEED THIS TO WORK.

THEN LEAVE ME TO *DO* MY WORK, TALUS.

AKASHA HAS TAKEN NORTH AFRICA FOR THE ORDO DRACUL, GRAND MASTER. CAIRO WAS OUR LAST HOLDOUT.

PARLIAMENT VOTED TO JOIN THE MOVEMENT TODAY.

WE'RE SEEING A RISE IN PRO-DRACULA SENTIMENT ACROSS THE EU AS WELL.

SIGNE HAS A TALENT FOR ROUSING THE RABBLE.

...AND ASIA?

NO WORD, GRAND MASTER.

IT'S BEEN RADIO SILENCE SINCE THE CCP MET WITH AKUMU SIX WEEKS AGO.

THANK YOU, BROTHERS. YOU ARE DISMISSED.

GRAND MASTER.

I PRAY YOU BRING ME GOOD TIDINGS, BROTHER TALUS.

I DO NOT, GRAND MASTER.

PROBLEM WITH YOUR SOLDIERS?

NO, GRAND MASTER. MY *PROBLEM* IS WITH THE WAR!

OR, PERHAPS I SHOULD SAY, THE LACK THEREOF.

BROTHER VICTOR?

HE'S A FRUSTRATING, ARROGANT SON OF A BITCH. BUT, HE'S BLOODY BRILLIANT.

IF ANY MAN CAN UNLOCK THE MYSTERIES OF THE UNDEAD, IT'S HIM.

I DON'T LIKE TO BE SPIED UPON. IT SUGGESTS A LACK OF TRUST.

TRUST IS EARNED, BROTHER.

DOCTOR. IT'S DOCTOR.

"I CAN ALREADY REANIMATE THE DEAD...

"...BUT I JUST CAN'T STOP THEM FROM EATING EVERYTHING IN SIGHT."

DRACULA WAS RIGHT. HUMANS ARE FUNDAMENTALLY *FLAWED!*

THANK YOU, BROTHER.

FUCK OFF!

KITTY-CAT ON A SECURE CHANNEL, GRAND MASTER.

PUT IT THROUGH.

AYE, SIR.

NACHASH IS ALONE. NOW IS THE TIME.

DANKE.

AYE, GRAND MASTER.

DĀBBAT AL-ARD!

DĀBBAT AL-ARD. REPEAT. DĀBBAT AL-ARD. ALL TEAMS. DĀBBAT AL-ARD.

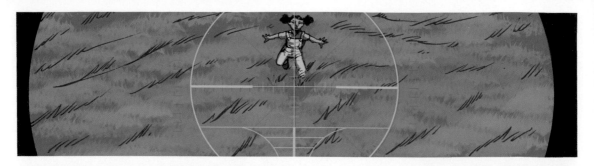

SHE'S NO BOTHER.

JONATHAN. ARTHUR. THIS IS ISAIAH.

HE'S THE OVERSEER OF THIS FARM, BUT MOLLY IS THE REAL BOSS 'ROUND THESE PARTS."

A PLEASURE.

MY FRIENDS NEED A SAFE PLACE TO STAY. WE HAVE ROOM RIGHT?

WE CAN'T IMPOSE...

PLENTY!

STAY AS LONG AS YOU'D NEED. LEAVE WHENEVER YOU'D LIKE. YOU'RE NOT PRISONERS HERE. NO ONE IS.

THIS ISN'T WHAT I EXPECTED.

WHAT *DID* YOU EXPECT?

I DON'T KNOW. SOMETHING MORE SCHINDLER'S LIST?

I'M A VAMPIRE, JONATHAN. I'M NOT A MONSTER.

I WON'T LIE TO YOU, JONATHAN. THIS IS A FARM. ONE OF MANY. THINGS HAPPEN HERE.

NECESSARY THINGS...BUT THINGS THAT YOU MAY FIND TROUBLING.

RISE OF DRACULA

CHAPTER FOUR

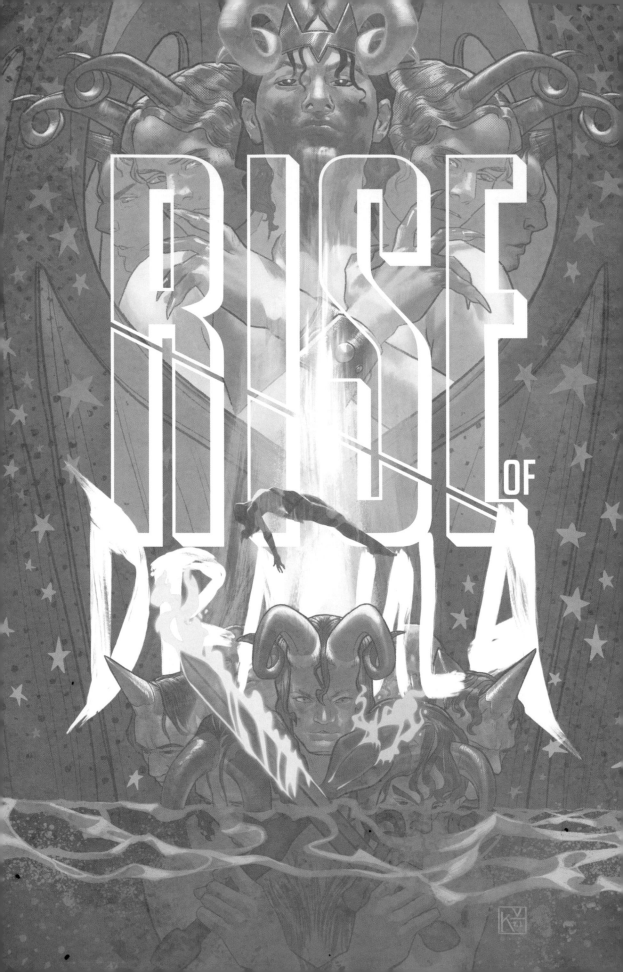

WE'RE BRINGING YOU LIVE COVERAGE OF DRACULA'S FUNERAL...

abc NEWS DRACULA'S FUNERAL 19:

COFFEE BEAN · COFFEE BEAN

CIT

...BORN WILHELMINA PATRICK MURRAY, THE CONTROVERSIAL REFORMER WAS ASSASSINATED WHILE LEADING A GOODWILL TOUR OF THE HILLINGHAM AGRICULTURAL COLLECTIVE.

HILLINGHAM IS ONE OF TEN RE-EDUCATION COMMUNES ESTABLISHED BY THE ORDO DRACUL TO HOUSE REFUGEES DISPLACED BY AMERICA'S WAR ON MARGINALIZED COMMUNITIES...

·LIVE

DRACULA'S MESSAGE REJECTING IDENTITY POLITICS RESONATED WITH FREEDOM FIGHTERS EVERYWHERE.

·LIVE

THE MOVEMENT IS FORCING OPPRESSOR NATIONS AROUND THE WORLD TO IMPLEMENT IMMEDIATE REFORMS...

CBS NEWS DRACULA'S MOURNERS 19:05

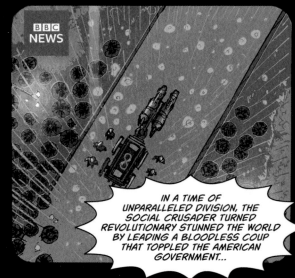

BBC NEWS

IN A TIME OF UNPARALLELED DIVISION, THE SOCIAL CRUSADER TURNED REVOLUTIONARY STUNNED THE WORLD BY LEADING A BLOODLESS COUP THAT TOPPLED THE AMERICAN GOVERNMENT...

·LIVE

DRACULA HAS FINALLY DELIVERED A CHANGE WE CAN BELIEVE IN.

Bloomberg NEWS

I CAN'T DO THIS.

YOU CAN, LOVE. I PROMISE.

WHEN I BECAME DRACULA...

I'M NOTHING LIKE YOU! YOU WERE BORN TO DO THIS. YOU WERE GROOMED TO BE DRACULA.

I WASN'T EVEN SUPPOSED TO HAPPEN! I SHOULDN'T BE HERE!

BUT YOU ARE HERE.

YOU DO EXIST AND YOU WILL DO THIS. YOU MUST.

IT'S NOT FAIR!

SHE'S RIGHT, MOTHER, IT ISN'T FAIR.

YOU'VE ALWAYS BEEN HER CHAMPION. YOUR LOVE FOR YOUR SISTER IS COMMENDABLE, BUT FOOLISH.

THE ABOMINATION SHOULD HAVE BEEN DROWNED THE MOMENT IT WAS BORN.

THERE CAN BE ONLY ONE DRACULA IN ANY AGE. SO IT IS WRITTEN.

WELL, NOW THERE IS. BECAUSE I'M...YOU KNOW... DEAD.

BLESSED BE!

HAIL DRACULA!

BLESSED BE!

UMM...HELLO... I'M SORRY. I REALLY HATE PUBLIC SPEAKING... I'M TERRIBLE AT IT...I'M SUPPOSED TO READ THIS SPEECH...

I'M SORRY, ABRAHAM, IT'S A GREAT SPEECH...I JUST...I'M JUST GOING TO SAY WHAT'S ON MY MIND...

I'M SORRY...I'M NOT SUPPOSED TO BE HERE...MY SISTER...BUT... SHE'S GONE...I'M DRACULA NOW...

WHEN I BECAME DRACULA, I ABSORBED THE MEMORIES AND EXPERIENCES OF EVERY WOMAN WHO HAS BORNE THIS LEGACY BEFORE ME.

HUNDREDS OF WOMEN HUNDREDS OF LIFETIMES.

IN ALL OF THOSE LIVES, WE HAVE LEARNED ONE INDISPUTABLE TRUTH: HUMANITY IS IRREDEEMABLE.

HUMANITY THREATENS ALL OF CREATION.

MARRY ME!

THERE ARE TOO MANY OF YOU...DEEP DOWN, YOU KNOW IT...YOU JUST WON'T ADMIT IT...YOU'RE KILLING THE WORLD... BLEEDING IT DRY...

IS THE WAY

MY SISTER LOVED YOU.

I DON'T.

I HATE YOU.

BUT I WILL SAVE YOU.

I LIKE TO READ. I LOVE MOVIES.

I READ ALL THESE BOOKS...WATCH ALL THESE MOVIES...ABOUT DYSTOPIAN SOCIETIES.

THEY'RE ALL PRETTY MUCH THE SAME.

AMERICA GREAT AGAIN!

SAVIOR

NOT MY DRACULA

THE GREEDY DID SOMETHING STUPID FOR...WELL...GREED.

IT FUCKED THE WORLD. ALL THE PEOPLE ARE SUFFERING UNDER THEIR OPPRESSION.

A HERO RISES UP FROM THE MASSES TO LEAD THE ENLIGHTENED OPPRESSED IN OVERTHROWING THEIR OPPRESSORS WHO STILL LIVE IN THE DARKNESS OF EXCESS, AVARICE AND GLUTTONY.

I FUCKING HATE THOSE STORIES.

YOU'RE SUPPOSED TO SEE IT AS THE TRIUMPH OF THE HUMAN SPIRIT EVEN AGAINST IMPOSSIBLE ODDS.

YOU'RE SUPPOSED TO APPRECIATE THE OPPORTUNITIES FOR THE FORMERLY OPPRESSED TO REMAKE THE WORLD IN A NEWER, KINDER, MORE EQUITABLE FASHION.

THAT'S NOT HOW I SEE IT.

THAT'S NOT WHAT HAPPENS.

YOU SEE, WHETHER IT'S A MOVIE OR A BOOK OR EVEN A VIDEO GAME...

...THE STORY ALWAYS ENDS AT THE EXACT MOMENT THE OPPRESSED TAKE THEIR FIRST STEPS TOWARD BECOMING THE OPPRESSORS.

THE OPPRESSORS DIDN'T START OPPRESSING THE MOMENT THEY BURST FROM THE WOMB.

FUCK...MOST OF THEM NEVER EVEN KNOW THEY'RE OPPRESSING ANYONE.

THEY NEVER INTENDED TO ENSLAVE THE WORLD.

THEY JUST LIVE THEIR LIVES THE BEST WAY THEY CAN...

...MAKING THE BEST DECISIONS FOR THEM AND FOR THOSE THEY HOLD DEAR.

THEY DIDN'T CHOOSE TO BE THE BAD GUYS.

THEY BECAME THE BAD GUYS BY THE CHOICES THAT THEY MADE.

SEE WHERE I'M GOING WITH THIS?

THOSE PEOPLE LIFTING THOSE OPPRESSIVE BOOTS TO CRAWL OUT FROM THOSE DEPRESSING GUTTERS ARE GOING TO SLIP THOSE SAME BOOTS ON...

...AND MARCH RIGHT INTO THE CATHEDRALS OF OPPRESSION RECENTLY VACATED BY THEIR NOW BAREFOOT PREDECESSORS BLEEDING OUT INTO THE GUTTERS.

THEY'LL LIVE THEIR LIVES AS BEST THEY CAN, MAKING THE BEST DECISIONS FOR THEM AND FOR THE PEOPLE THEY HOLD DEAR.

IN A GENERATION OR TWO OR THREE OR SIX OR TEN THE YLIGHT OF THE NOUVEAU OPPRIMEE WILL ECHO AGAIN FROM THE GUTTERS.

THEY'LL REPEAT THIS CYCLE UNTIL THE SUN DEVOURS THE WORLD MAKING THEM ALL IRRELEVANT AGAIN.

I MAKE NO PRETENSIONS ABOUT BEING THE GOOD GUY. I'M NOT MY SISTER.

IF YOU ARE A PRODUCTIVE MEMBER OF SOCIETY, AN APP IS NOW BEING INSTALLED ON YOUR MOBILE DEVICE.

IT GRANTS YOU UNFETTERED ACCESS TO FOOD, SHELTER, MEDICINE, EDUCATION. EVERYTHING YOU NEED TO LIVE A FULFILLING, PEACEFUL LIFE.

IF YOU DO NOT RECEIVE THIS APP, YOU HAVE BEEN IDENTIFIED AS A BURDEN TO SOCIETY.

YOU WILL BE REMANDED TO THE NEAREST PROCESSING FACILITY.

THERE YOU WILL BE ASSESSED FOR ANY POTENTIAL VALUE YOU MIGHT HAVE.

I DON'T CARE WHO LIVES OR WHO DIES.

I'M EQUALLY DEAF TO THOSE WHO SUFFER AND THOSE WHO THRIVE.

I WANT THEM ALL TO BURN BECAUSE I'M BORED WALKING AROUND IN CIRCLES.

BLESSED BE.

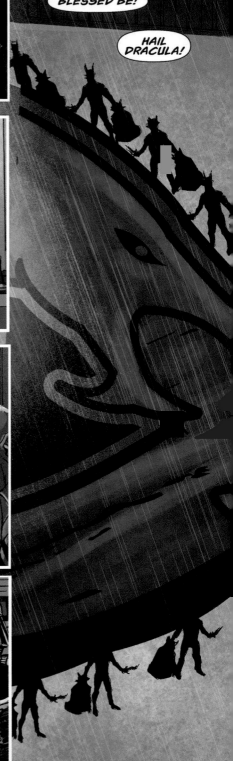

HAIL DRACULA!

BLESSED BE!

HAIL DRACULA!

BLESSED BE!

IN AMERICA ONE OUT OF EVERY SEVEN CHILDREN LIVES WITH FOOD INSECURITY. THIRTEEN MILLION CHILDREN. *STARVING.*

THAT'S A DISGRACE. IT IS PROOF THAT HUMANITY IS NOT FIT TO BE FREE.

IF THE WEALTHIEST AND MOST PROSPEROUS NATION THE WORLD HAS EVER KNOWN CANNOT FEED ITS OWN CHILDREN...

...HOW CAN LESS PRIVILEGED NATIONS BE EXPECTED TO DO SO? *THEY CAN'T.*

DRACULA BRINGS HOPE TO A HOPELESS WORLD.

NO PERSON UNDER DRACULA'S PROTECTION WILL SUFFER NEEDLESSLY FROM TREATABLE DISEASE.

THE THINGS WE HAVE ACHIEVED HERE IN DC WILL FLOURISH AROUND THE WORLD.

WE *WILL* LEAVE NO CHILD BEHIND.

WE *WILL* ELIMINATE FOOD INSECURITY AND HOUSING INSTABILITY.

OUR ANTI-POVERTY INITIATIVES ARE THE CORNERSTONES OF OUR FAITH.

THEY ARE WHY HUNDREDS OF THOUSANDS OF GOOD, HONEST, SALT OF THE EARTH PEOPLE HAVE JOINED OUR MOVEMENT.

THE PEOPLE TRUST DRACULA BECAUSE THEY KNOW SHE WILL DO THE THINGS THEY CANNOT BRING THEMSELVES TO DO.

EVEN IF THEY KNOW THEY'RE RIGHT.

QUESTIONS?

MINISTER!

HOW DO YOU ANSWER CLAIMS THAT DRACULA'S ACTIONS ARE ILLEGAL IN A DEMOCRACY? DON'T HER INITIATIVES VIOLATE HUMAN RIGHTS AND LIBERTIES?

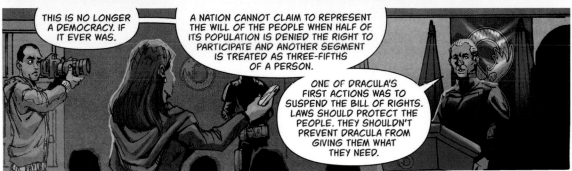

THIS IS NO LONGER A DEMOCRACY. IF IT EVER WAS.

A NATION CANNOT CLAIM TO REPRESENT THE WILL OF THE PEOPLE WHEN HALF OF ITS POPULATION IS DENIED THE RIGHT TO PARTICIPATE AND ANOTHER SEGMENT IS TREATED AS THREE-FIFTHS OF A PERSON.

ONE OF DRACULA'S FIRST ACTIONS WAS TO SUSPEND THE BILL OF RIGHTS. LAWS SHOULD PROTECT THE PEOPLE. THEY SHOULDN'T PREVENT DRACULA FROM GIVING THEM WHAT THEY NEED.

YOU SAY THAT DRACULA WILL LEAVE NO ONE BEHIND. THAT DOESN'T SEEM TO GEL WITH HER CONCENTRATION CAMPS.

EVERYONE TAKEN TO OUR **PROCESSING CENTERS** IS THOROUGHLY EVALUATED AND GIVEN EVERY OPPORTUNITY TO BE A BENEFIT TO SOCIETY. OUR DOCTORS TREAT THEIR AILMENTS.

WE PROVIDE WORLD CLASS EDUCATION AND JOB TRAINING. WE GIVE THEM EVERY TOOL NECESSARY TO BE PRODUCTIVE MEMBERS OF SOCIETY. **EVERYONE** MUST CONTRIBUTE IN SOME WAY.

YOU SAY THAT EVERYONE MUST CONTRIBUTE IN SOME WAY.

WHAT HAPPENS TO THOSE WHO **CAN'T?**

HUMANS EXPEND FAR TOO MUCH TIME AND RESOURCES CATERING TO THE NEEDS OF THE EXTREME.

THE EXTREMELY WEALTHY GET ALL OF THE ECONOMIC BREAKS.

THE EXTREMELY POOR SUCK UP ALL THE SOCIAL RESOURCES.

DRACULA'S FOCUS IS ON THE VAST MAJORITY OF THE PEOPLE WHO LAND SOMEWHERE IN BETWEEN.

YES, THAT DOES MEAN THAT THE WORLD WILL MOVE ON WITHOUT SOME PEOPLE. THERE WILL BE FAR FEWER THAN WERE IGNORED BY THE PREVIOUS REGIME.

THANK YOU ALL. NO FURTHER QUESTIONS.

A BIT EARLY ISN'T IT?

LATE. EARLY. I HAVE NO **FUCKING** IDEA, ELIZABETH.

I'VE BEEN IN THIS CAVE FOR MONTHS.

WHAT'S WRONG?

I CAN'T CRACK THEIR GENOME. THEY'RE HUMAN, BUT THEY'RE NOT.

THEY REPRODUCE BY PASSING THEIR GENETIC INFORMATION THROUGH DNA IN THEIR SALIVA. THEY ESSENTIALLY CLONE THEMSELVES WHEN THEY BITE.

THE DNA LIES DORMANT...SOMETIMES FOR YEARS, DECADES EVEN...THEN ONE DAY IT JUST MAGICALLY ACTIVATES. I HAVE NO IDEA HOW OR WHY.

YOU'LL FIGURE IT OUT.

I HOPE SO.

THEY'LL KILL YOU IF YOU DON'T.

I KNOW.

VROOOOM

KRUNK

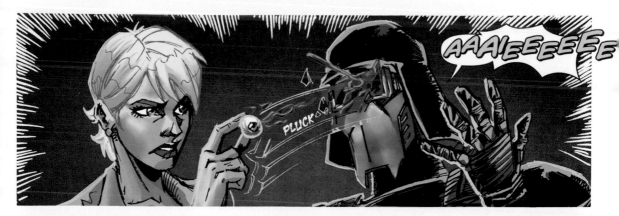

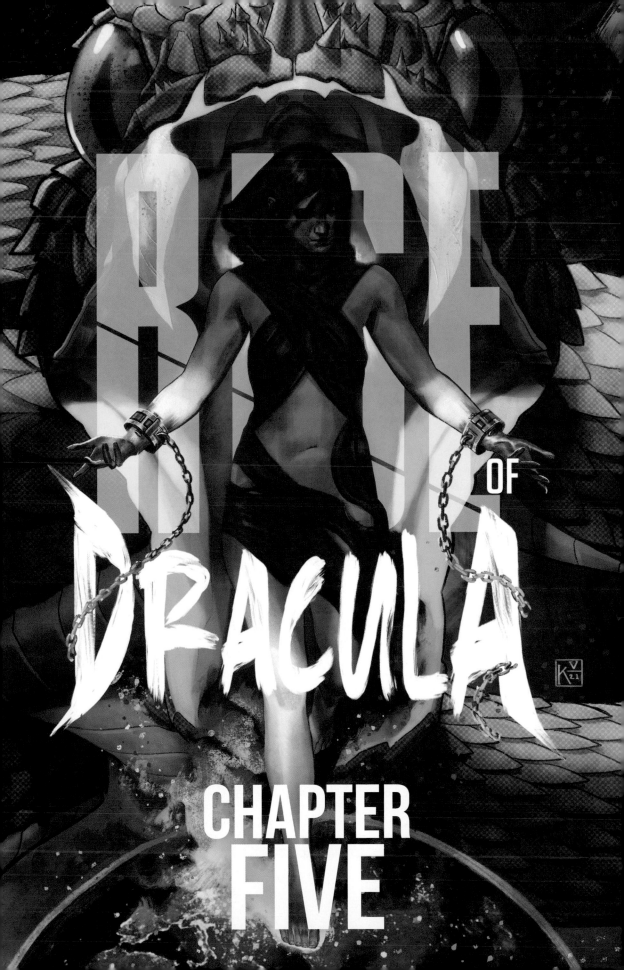

RISE OF DRACULA

CHAPTER FIVE

RISE

OF

DRACULA

Woodland Park
Re-Education
Center

♪ OUR EYES HAVE SEEN THE GLORY OF OUR SAVIOR DRACULA. SHE IS ROOTING OUT CORRUPTION AND WILL SEE OUR WORLD RESTORED. ♪

♪ SHE WILL GUIDE US TO THE FUTURE WITH ENSURED PROSPERITY. HER TRUTH IS MARCHING ON! ♪

PROSPERITY MEANS MANY THINGS TO MANY PEOPLE.

THE ORDER GUARANTEES THE STABILITY, SECURITY AND SUSTAINABILITY TO ALL CITIZENS CONTRIBUTING TO OUR NEW GREAT SOCIETY.

THESE PROMISES ARE GIVEN FREELY, BUT THEY ARE NOT GIVEN WITHOUT COST.

GREAT ACHIEVEMENTS REQUIRE GREAT COMMITMENT.

EVERY GOOD CITIZEN MUST REMAIN STEADFAST AGAINST THE CORRUPTIVE INFLUENCE OF DEVIANTS AND DEFECTIVES.

TALK TO YOUR PARENTS. TALK TO YOUR TEACHERS.

THEY'LL SHOW YOU HOW TO SPOT A DEFECTIVE OR A DEVIANT!

♪ GLORY! GLORY! PEACE IN DRACULA! BY HER GRACE WE WILL PROSPER! GLORY! GLORY! TO THE ORDER! OUR WILL IS MARCHING ON! ♪

WHAT *IS* A DEVIANT? WHAT MAKES A PERSON DEFECTIVE?

CAN YOU THINK OF AN EXAMPLE?

A *DUM-DUM?*

THAT'S RIGHT, DIEGO! *DUM-DUMS* MAKE IT HARDER FOR TREYVON TO ACHIEVE HIS FULL ACADEMIC POTENTIAL.

EVERYONE CAN ACHIEVE MORE WITHOUT THE DISTRACTIONS OF DUM-DUMS WHO CAN'T KEEP UP! DUM-DUMS DRAG US ALL DOWN BECAUSE THEY CAN'T.

EVERY MINUTE THAT A TEACHER IS DISTRACTED BY A DUM-DUM IS A MOMENT STOLEN FROM EACH OF YOU. THAT'S NOT FAIR, IS IT?

NOOOOOOO!

BUT WHAT IF IT'S NOT THEIR FAULT? WHAT IF THEY DON'T MEAN TO BE A DUM-DUM?

WHAT IF THEY HAVE A DISABILITY THAT MAKES THEM DUMB?

THAT'S A GREAT QUESTION, RIKKU!

CLASS? DOES ANYONE KNOW THE ANSWER TO RIKKU'S QUESTION?

CRIMINALS AND THUGS!

PEOPLE WHO REFUSE TO WORK!

PEOPLE WHO DON'T SUPPORT THE ORDER!

ANTI-VAXXERS!

WE'VE ALREADY COVERED DUM-DUMS, PIPER.

MINISTER VAN HELSING?

YES, BRIANNA?

WHAT DOES PROCESSING MEAN?

THANK YOU FOR ASKING SUCH A WONDERFUL QUESTION!

YOU'RE WELCOME!

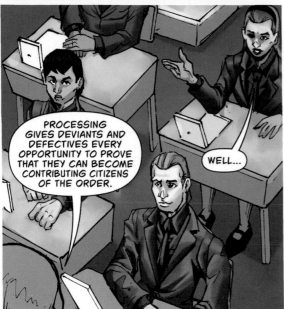

PROCESSING GIVES DEVIANTS AND DEFECTIVES EVERY OPPORTUNITY TO PROVE THAT THEY CAN BECOME CONTRIBUTING CITIZENS OF THE ORDER.

WELL...

...WHAT HAPPENS IF THEY CAN'T BE CONTRIBUTORS?

THEY'RE SENT TO THE FARMS.

WHAT DO THEY DO THERE?

LET'S SAY THAT THERE IS ONE WAY THAT EVERYONE CAN CONTRIBUTE AND LEAVE IT THERE SHALL WE?

UUURRRRMMMKK

≑SIGH≑

ISAIAH? WHAT'S ON YOUR MIND SON?

NOTHIN' MAMA.

NO NEED TO BE PROUD AROUND ME, CHILD! I RAISED YOU. I WIPED YOUR TEARS *AND* YOUR ASS.

NOTHIN' LEFT TO HIDE FROM ME. MAMA'S SEEN IT *ALL*.

THINKING ABOUT SNEAKING OFF. TAKING MOLLY. MAKING A NEW START OUT WEST.

FREE STATES?

MMMMHMMM.

THINKING ABOUT JOINING THE RESISTANCE?

NAW! MINA WAS GOOD TO US WHEN SHE WAS DRACULA. WOULDN'T BE RIGHT TO STAB HER IN THE BACK NOW.

EVEN IF SHE IS DEAD.

HEARD YOU SAY YOU'RE TAKING MOLLY WITH YOU. DIDN'T HEAR YOU MENTION AYA'S NAME.

SHE AIN'T GONNA GO.

SHE AIN'T GONNA LET YOU GO. NOT WITH HER CHILD.

THAT'S WHY I SAID I WAS SNEAKING OFF. I DON'T PLAN ON GIVING HER A VOICE ON THE MATTER.

SHE'S YOUR WIFE, ISAIAH. HER VOICE ISN'T YOURS TO GIVE.

YOU'VE MADE A GOOD LIFE HERE, SON. WORK'S UNPLEASANT BUT YOU DO WHAT YOU'VE GOTTA DO FOR YOUR FAMILY.

YOU PUT A ROOF OVER THEIR HEAD AND FOOD IN THEIR BELLY.

A LOT OF FATHERS PROVIDE A LOT LESS.

YOU'RE A GOOD MAN, ISAIAH, EVEN IF YOU'VE GOTTA DO SOME BAD THINGS.

YOU THINK LONG AND HARD BEFORE YOU GO RUNNING OFF AFTER SOMETHING THAT MIGHT NOT BE THERE.

I WILL.

PROMISE?

I PROMISE.

PROMISE.

I SAID I PROMISE, MAMA.

THAT'S THREE TIMES YOU PROMISED. THAT'S A SACRED VOW.

SCHIK

I'D NEVER LIE TO YOU. NOT TO DELTHEA THE HOODOO PRIESTESS. DAMNED SURE NOT TO MY MAMA!

I LOVE YOU, ISAIAH.

I LOVE YOU TOO, MAMA.

YOU GOT WORK TO DO, SON. BEST GET TO DOIN IT.

RECKON I SHOULD.

WALK WITH ME A BIT?

ALWAYS.

WE'RE WELL UNDER WAY AND SHE'S FAR EXCEEDING OUR EXPECTATIONS. SHE'S NOT EVEN BOTHERING TO SORT THE WHEAT FROM THE CHAFF.

YOU'LL HAVE YOUR MONSTER BY MORNING, LADY RUTHVEN.

SHE'S MAD, CARMILLA.

SHE'S ALREADY A MONSTER. WE NEED ONLY SHOW THAT TO THE WORLD.

I BELIEVE THAT'S MY DEPARTMENT.

IT'S ALL BEEN ARRANGED. THE 'NERO NARRATIVE' IS SET TO GO LIVE ON ALL SOCIAL MEDIA OUTLETS BY YOUR COMMAND, LADY RUTHVEN.

ONCE UPON A TIME, ONE NEEDED AN ARMY TO SACK A CITY.

NOW ONE PERSON CAN TOPPLE AN EMPIRE FROM THE PALM OF HER HAND.

ARMIES STILL HAVE THEIR PLACE IN REVOLUTIONS. OURS WILL BE READY WHEN THE TIME COMES.

HUWAKK

I'M DYING.

YOU'RE NOT DYING. YOU'RE JUST PURGING ALL THAT PURE CONCENTRATED EVIL.

I ONLY HAD ONE WHITE CLAW.

IT WAS PUMPKIN SPICE, WASN'T IT?

YES...

WE WERE JUST IN TIME.

ANY LATER AND OUR BELOVED SISTER WOULD BE...GONE.

HU

LOST TO THE REALM OF BASIC WHITE BITCHES FOREVER.

WANDERING ETERNITY IN UGGS, LEGGINGS A PUFFER VEST AND THAT GODAWFUL MESSY PONYTAIL!

I DUNNO. I THINK SHE'D LOOK CUTE WITH A MESSY PONYTAIL.

IS THERE ANYTHING YOU DON'T LOOK GOOD IN?

THE TOILET?

NOPE! HEAD HUNG IN THE TOILET IN A ROLLER DISCO STRIP CLUB IN HELL...

...VOMIT RUNNING DOWN YOUR CHIN, FACE WET FROM PISS WATER AND I'LL BET YOU CAN STILL CATCH A DICK!

YEAH, BUT GUYS ARE EASY.

I COULD CATCH A DICK TONIGHT IF I WANTED...AND I DON'T EVEN HAVE A BODY.

GOT DEM LIPS THO.

WUB WUB WUB

SURELY THAT'S NOT IT, RIGHT? THERE'S MORE? I DON'T WANT TO BE FORGOTTEN LIKE THIS.

AWWW! HONEY! OF COURSE THERE'S MORE. JUST BECAUSE YOU HAVEN'T DONE ANYTHING YET DOESN'T MEAN YOU WON'T.

I'D HUG YOU RIGHT NOW ELLIE, BUT...I WELL...NO HANDS.

WANNA GO DOWN TO CHARON'S MARINA?

TORMENT THE NEW ARRIVALS?

UH HUH.

WANNA PRETEND WE'LL MAKE OUT WITH THEM BUT THEN LOCK THEM IN THAT CREEPY ROOM AT THE END OF THE HALL WHERE I SAW THAT THREE HEADED DOG THING?

HELL YEAH!

RISE OF DRACULA

CHAPTER SIX

"BEHOLD, THE PEOPLE RISE
LIKE A LIONESS; THEY
ROUSE THEMSELVES LIKE A
LION, NOT RESTING UNTIL
THEY DEVOUR THEIR PREY
AND DRINK THE BLOOD OF
THE SLAIN."

NUMBERS 23:24

The White House
Rose Garden

Damaskinos

Damaskinos

WELL HELLO, YOUNG MAN.

HELLO.

MIND IF I SIT A SPELL?

NO.

MY NAME IS DELTHEA. MAY I ASK YOURS?

ROONE.

ISN'T THAT AN INTERESTING NAME.

I GUESS SO.

WHAT ARE YOU DOING IN HERE ALL ALONE, MR. ROONE?

I'M NOT SURE. SOME MEN CAME TO MY HOUSE AND TOOK ME TO A FARM. I SAW COWS AND CHICKENS AND DUCKS.

THEY LET ME PET THE DOG. HIS NAME WAS TAZ BECAUSE HE'S SO CRAZY.

THEN SOME OTHER MEN CAME AND BROUGHT ME HERE. THEY SAID I COULD BE USEFUL.

I WANTED TO HELP. MAMA SAYS IT'S ALWAYS GOOD TO BE HELPFUL. HELPFUL MEANS ALMOST THE SAME AS USEFUL. MAYBE IF I'M A HELPER, I CAN GO HOME AND MAMA WON'T CRY ANYMORE.

SHE WAS SAD WHEN THE MEN TOOK ME AWAY.

I DIDN'T MEAN TO MAKE MAMA CRY.

OH SWEET CHILD. LITTLE BOYS ALWAYS MAKE MOTHERS CRY, BUT IT'S NOT YOUR FAULT.

SHE JUST LOVES YOU SO MUCH SHE CAN'T HOLD IT IN.

NOW YOU LISTEN TO GRANNY DELTHEA, YOU HEAR?

YOUR MAMA LOVES YOU. YOU'RE A GOOD BOY.

A BRAVE BOY. YOUR MAMA IS PROUD OF YOU.

YOU *WILL* SEE HER AGAIN.

BYE, GRANNY DELTHEA. I'M GONNA GO BE A HELPER NOW!

GOODBYE, ROONE. DON'T FORGET WHAT I SAID.

YOU ARE A GOOD BOY. YOU ARE LOVED.

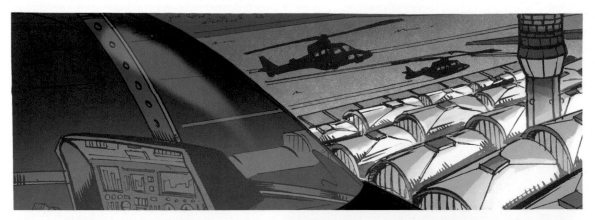

RIGHT THIS WAY, LADY RUTHVEN.

NYARNG
NYARNG
NYARNG

TSSSS

SKITCH
SKITCH

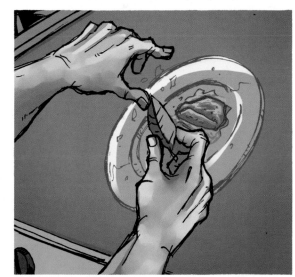

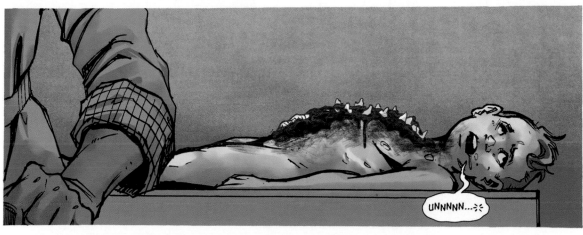

UNNNNN...

DON'T BE AFRAID.

I'M NO VULCAN, BUT THE LOGIC HERE IS PRETTY CLEAR.

THE NEEDS OF THE MANY DO INDEED OUTWEIGH THE NEEDS OF THE FEW.

AAA!

"AREN'T *WE* THE FEW?"

OH NO, MARK. WE'RE *THE ONLY.*

"THE ONLY ONES THAT MATTER ANYWAY."

YOU SHOULD COME WORK FOR ME.

"HARD PASS."

I ONLY WORK FOR VAMPIRES I CAN TRUST.

RRIIIP

GRRARGH

RRAH!

AAAACK!

SHICK

GET THEM!

WHUP WHUP WHUP

BRAKKA BRAKKA BRAKKA BRAKKA BRAKKA BRAKKA SPLUT SPLUT SPLUT SPLUT

GRAHHH!

BRAKKA BRAKKA BRAKKA BRAKKA

SKRAK

KABOOM

GASP